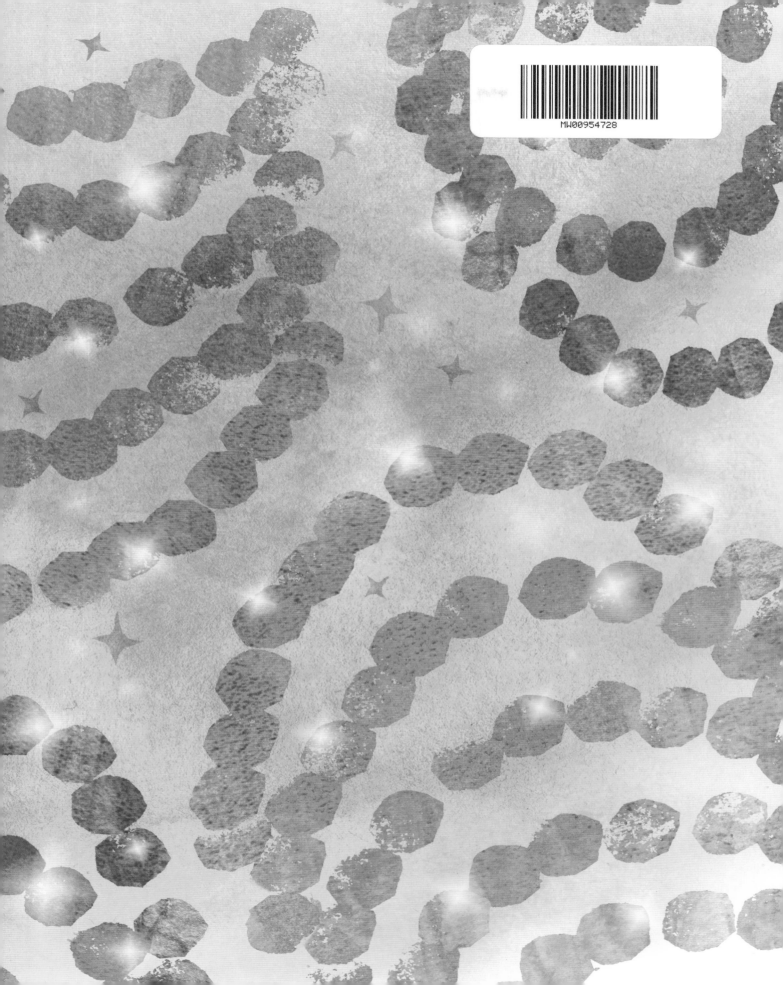

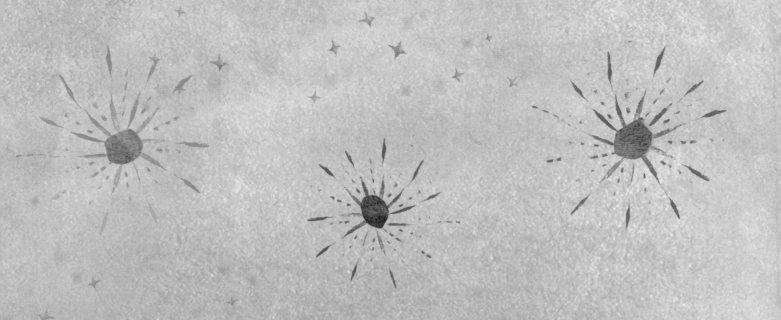

To Duncan, with love.
— *Heather Smith*

For Ella Jane, who glows so bright!
— *Alice Carter*

Angus All Aglow

HEATHER SMITH ★ ALICE CARTER

Angus liked

sparkly

things.

The rainbow sequins on his sister's tutu.

The sun's reflection on Baker Lake in summer.
The diamond studs on the collar of his dog, Sherlock.

Angus liked sparkly **words** too.

Lustrous
rolled off his tongue.

Scintillating

made his eyebrows dance.

Just saying the word **gleaming**

made his mouth smile.

Glistening was his favorite, because hidden in *glistening* is *listening*, and Angus liked sparkly things so much he felt as though he could hear them.

The nighttime stars crackled like a campfire.

The metal taps on his sister's dance shoes

whiz-BANG-popped
like fireworks.

His sapphire-studded scissors sizzled
like frying bacon.

Angus's favorite sparkly thing of all was Grandma June's necklace. It had five strands of colorful glass beads that sounded like popcorn being popped in a metal pot.

One day Grandma June noticed Angus admiring her necklace. She slipped it over his head.

"It's all yours," she said.

Angus felt a twinkling deep inside his belly.
It was his inner sparkle, fizzy and warm.
Angus glowed from the inside out.

The next morning Angus decided to wear Grandma June's necklace to school.

His sister said, "Angus, that necklace doesn't really match the rest of your outfit. Why don't you wear a scarf instead?"

Angus said, "Scarves don't sparkle."

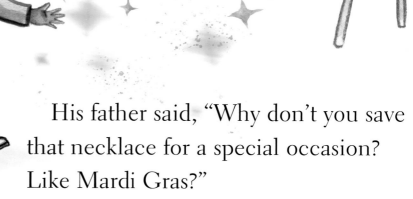

His father said, "Why don't you save that necklace for a special occasion? Like Mardi Gras?"

Angus said, "Why can't every day be Mardi Gras?"

His mother said, "Angus, the thing is, that necklace is… really bright."

Angus said, "That's the point."

Heads turned as Angus walked into his classroom.
Could they hear the popping too?
Johnny Cole put his face in his hands and yelled,
"My eyes! My eyes!"

Others joined in. "Too bright! Too bright!"
Brett Andrews said, "Sparkles, Angus? Sparkles?"

His classmates' laughter was like a
downpour of freezing rain.

Angus ran into the hallway, where his inner sparkle fizzled like a wet firecracker.

He tried to pull the necklace over his head, but the strands twisted together. A thick loop got caught on his ear.

Angus yanked hard.

The glass beads seemed to lose their color as they bounced off the floor. The only sound Angus could hear was a shower of sad **plinkety-plinks**.

Just then Melody Daniels appeared. As she stepped into
the hallway her foot bumped a lone bead.

It rolled toward Angus.

It seemed to move in slow motion.

Angus and Melody followed it with their eyes.

They watched as it rolled to a
wibbly-wobbly stop
against the rubber sole of Angus's sneaker.
Angus frowned and kicked the bead away.
Then, turning his back on Melody,
he walked back into the classroom.

That night Angus went to his sister's dance recital.
Tap shoes glimmered and sequins shimmered.
But Angus didn't hear a whiz, a bang or a pop.

At bedtime Sherlock snuggled in close. But the diamond studs on his collar jabbed and poked. Angus pushed Sherlock away.

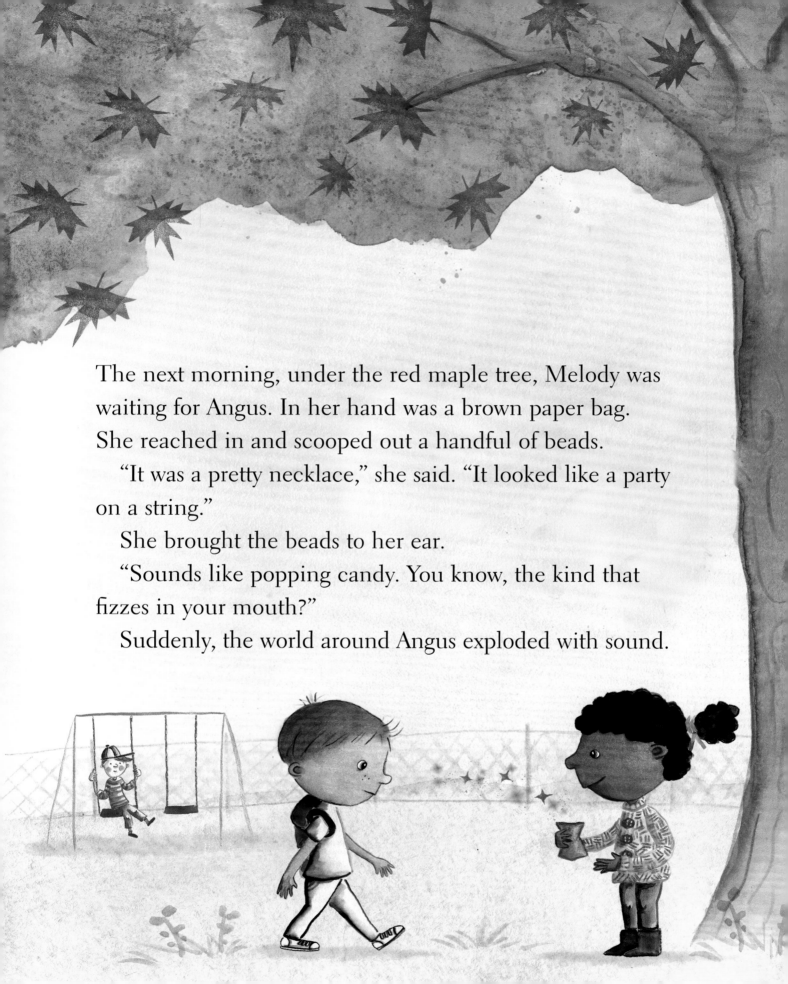

The next morning, under the red maple tree, Melody was waiting for Angus. In her hand was a brown paper bag. She reached in and scooped out a handful of beads.

"It was a pretty necklace," she said. "It looked like a party on a string."

She brought the beads to her ear.

"Sounds like popping candy. You know, the kind that fizzes in your mouth?"

Suddenly, the world around Angus exploded with sound.

The beads in Melody's hands **crick-crack-popped** like hot corn kernels.

The ruby buttons on her cardigan **buzzed** like a bazillion fireflies.

The rainbow ribbons in her hair cling-clang-rang like a parade.

The two friends sat together, admiring the beads while the leaves of the red maple sizzled above them.

Melody pulled a ribbon from her hair.
"Maybe you can make a new necklace."
Angus had a better idea.

With his sapphire-studded scissors, he snipped the ribbon
in two and threaded beads onto each piece.
He struggled to tie the ends.

"I can help," said Melody.

Together, they made two new bracelets.

Angus passed one to Melody. "It's all yours."

Melody beamed.

Angus clutched the second bracelet in his hand.
His fingers tingled as the beads hummed with
happiness. But underneath the thrum-thrum-thrum,
Angus could hear a dark whisper. *My eyes! My eyes!*
Too bright! Too bright!

His inner sparkle quivered like a flickering flame.
Melody reached out and touched the bracelet.
"It matches your outfit perfectly," she said.

The dark whisper disappeared like
a wisp of smoke on the breeze.
    Angus slipped the bracelet over his hand.
    The beads zizzle-zazzle-zapped
like lightning in a stormy sky.

Every head turned as Angus and Melody walked into the classroom.

Angus

glowed

from the inside out.

Cataloguing in Publication information available from Library and Archives Canada

Issued in print and electronic formats.
ISBN 978-1-4598-1493-6 (hardcover).—ISBN 978-1-4598-1494-3 (pdf).—
ISBN 978-1-4598-1495-0 (epub)

First published in the United States, 2018
Library of Congress Control Number: 2018933708

Summary: In this illustrated picture book, a young child can hear color
and is enamored with his grandmother's beaded necklace.

Orca Book Publishers is dedicated to preserving the environment and has printed this book on Forest Stewardship Council® certified paper.

Orca Book Publishers gratefully acknowledges the support for its publishing programs provided by the following agencies: the Government of Canada through the Canada Book Fund and the Canada Council for the Arts, and the Province of British Columbia through the BC Arts Council and the Book Publishing Tax Credit.

Cover and interior artwork created using watercolor, gouache and pencil.

Edited by Liz Kemp
Cover and interior artwork by Alice Carter
Design by Jenn Playford

ORCA BOOK PUBLISHERS
orcabook.com

Printed and bound in China.

21 20 19 18 • 4 3 2 1

Heather Smith

Originally from Newfoundland, Heather Smith now lives in Waterloo, Ontario, with her husband and three children. Her first novel, *Baygirl*, received a starred review from *Quill & Quire*. Angus was inspired by Heather's own child, who from a very young age told his parents that he attributed certain colors to letters and numbers and often went to school looking very dapper in a tartan bow tie. For more information, visit heathertsmith.com.

Alice Carter

Alice Carter has always loved telling stories through her whimsical art. A graduate of the Ontario College of Art and Design, she has worked as a freelance illustrator and fine artist for over ten years. She is inspired by people-watching, music and all the earth's magnificent creatures. Alice lives with her family of silly humans and serious cats in Ottawa, Ontario. For more information, visit alicecarter.com.

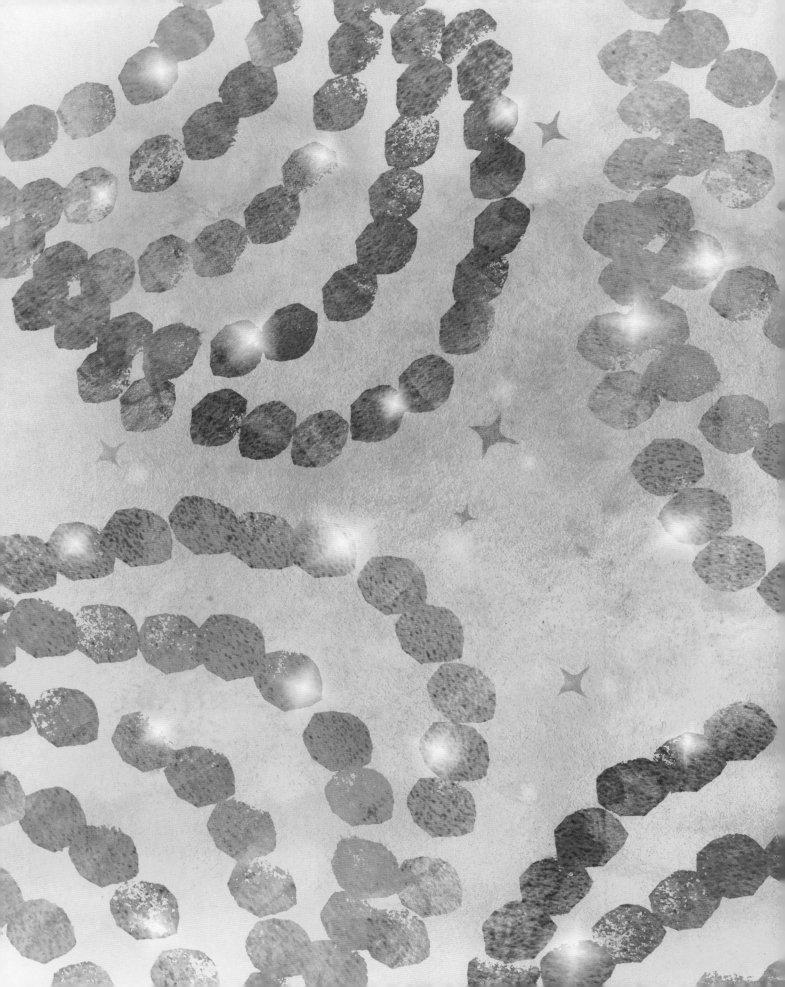